THE YETI FILES

Meet the Bigfeet

Scholastic Children's Books
An imprint of Scholastic Ltd
Euston House, 24 Eversholt Street
London, NW1 1DB, UK
Registered office: Westfield Road, Southam, Warwickshire, CV47 0RA
SCHOLASTIC and associated logos are trademarks and/or registered trademarks of Scholastic Inc.

First published in the US by Scholastic Inc, 2014
This edition published by Scholastic Ltd, 2014

Copyright © Kevin Sherry, 2014

The right of Kevin Sherry to be identified as the author
of this work has been asserted by him.

ISBN 978 1407 15202 8

A CIP catalogue record for this book is available from the British Library.

Printed and bound by CPI Group (UK) Ltd, Croydon, CR0 4YY
Papers used by Scholastic Children's Books are made from
wood grown in sustainable forests.

1 3 5 7 9 10 8 6 4 2

www.scholastic.co.uk

Thanks to Teresa Kietlinski, Bill Stevenson, Nolen Strals, Ryan Patterson, Ed Schrader, Dina Kelberman, Alan Resnick, Ben O'Brien, Bob O'Brien, Dan Deacon, Eduardo Lino Costa, Emily Wexler, Matt Gemmell, the Black Cherry Puppet Theater, Baltimore, and especially to my huge awesome family and my parents.

For Brian

Chapter 1:
I'M A YETI

Hi there!
I'm Blizz Richards.
And I'm a yeti.
Nice to meet you!

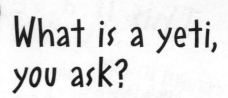

What is a yeti, you ask?

Is a yeti a man?

Not quite.

Is a yeti an ape?

Nope.

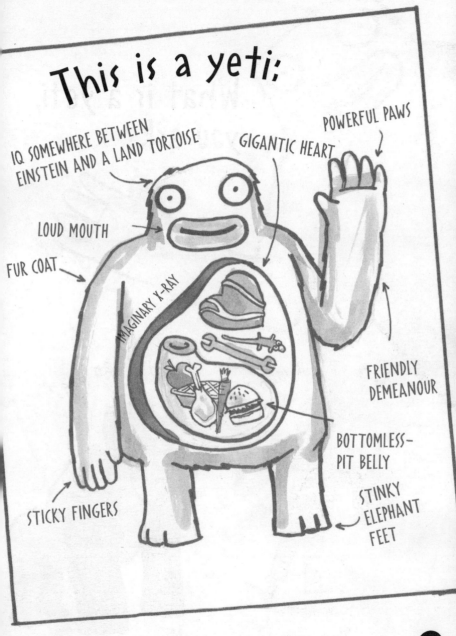

This is a yeti;

IQ SOMEWHERE BETWEEN EINSTEIN AND A LAND TORTOISE

GIGANTIC HEART

POWERFUL PAWS

LOUD MOUTH

FUR COAT

IMAGINARY X-RAY

FRIENDLY DEMEANOUR

BOTTOMLESS-PIT BELLY

STICKY FINGERS

STINKY ELEPHANT FEET

CHINA

NEPAL

INDIA

It's cold up here, so it's a good thing that I've got this nice fur coat. This is the entrance to my lair, my headquarters. I've got everything I need down here at HQ...

Bbrrrrrrrrr!!

flip!

¼ SCALE MODEL, BLUE WHALE

UNDERWATER AIRLOCK

CRYPTO OATH

T. REX SKELETON

TYRE SWING

WORKSHOP

TRAMPOLINE

6

UNFINISHED CHISELLING PROJECT

CINEMA

BRUCE LEE THE BABOON

CRYSTAL CAVE

ALL OF MY COMICS AND BEST BOOKS

THINKING CHAIR

CRYPTOTRON

BLIZZ RICHARDS SIGNED IN

RAT KING AT TACO SHACK

JERSEY DEVIL - I LOVE CANOEING

SUPERCOMPUTER

ROCK CLIMBING WALL

HOT TUB

I'm a yeti and that's a cryptid. A cryptid is a
hidden animal whose existence has never been proven.

We have all taken a powerful oath to never be seen by the outside world. The secrecy keeps magic and mystery in the minds of humans. And we all know how important that is.

Many different cryptids live all around the world.

UNICORN

ZOMBIE

YETI

MOTHMAN

MERMAID

VAMPIRE

SEWER CROC

LOCH NESS MONSTER

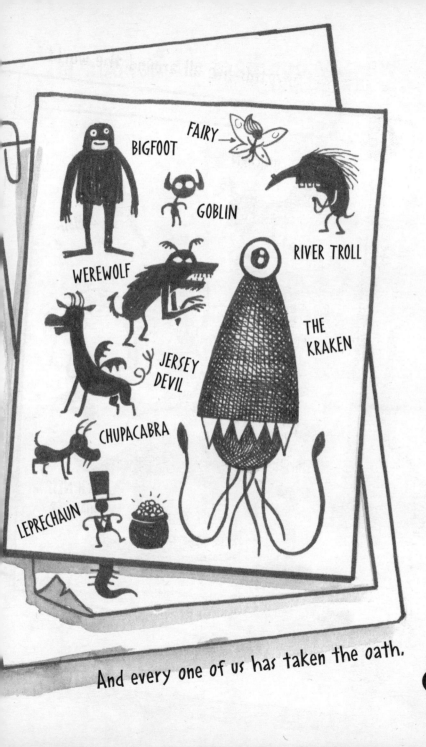

And every one of us has taken the oath.

We try our best to honour it.

Chapter 2:
AN INVITATION

I haven't got one of these in years! Gather around, buddies... We used to have these family reunions all the time ... and boy, were they fun!

This handsome fellow's name is Brian. He's my cousin, but he's also a lot like my brother.

We grew up together.

Brian loves all animals.

He is super strong and is a great cook.

INCREDIBLY POWERFUL TELESCOPE

HIGHLY POLISHED FIREMAN'S POLE

RATTLING DUNE BUGGY

ZIPPY ZIP LINE

BOUNCY TRAMPOLINE

COOKOUT CENTRAL

ORGANIC VEGETABLE GARDEN

We used to have a big party every year at Brian's awesome pad in Canada.

NETWORK OF LADDERS

VOLLEYBALL COURT

BUBBLING HOT TUB

EPIC TYRE SWING

BASKETBALL NET FOR SICK DUNKS

CHARBROIL SMOKER

But then Brian got **caught.**
Someone snapped his photo.

And soon the photo was everywhere.

Brian turned on his computer, and he saw that his picture was all over the entire Internet.

He was **mortified.** He had betrayed the cryptid oath. He couldn't bear to be seen ever again!

So Brian disappeared...

And it was all because of George Vanquist!

Chapter 3:
THE BAD GUY AND HIS DOG

TOO MUCH CONFIDENCE

George Vanquist

PRIZED MOUSTACHE

CLUELESS

CHOCOLATE

TROPHY TO HIMSELF

Noodles

146 IQ

CARGO SHORTS

GOOD SNIFFER

SECRET GENIUS

GEORGE VANQUIST
NEW BOOK

The photos George Vanquist took of Brian made George famous. He calls himself a cryptozoologist.

Ha!

"THE PHOTO"

BOOK
$20
SIGNED BOOK
$40

ME!

He tours for a living, doing school assemblies, motivational speeches, cocker spaniel conventions and any other gig he can get.

Whoops!
Looks like a slide from my Jamaican vacation.

But he just doesn't get it!

Cryptozoology is not about fame at all. It's about the honour and secrecy of members. Cryptozoology is about retaining our magic, not about revealing us to the public!

He'll do anything to prove we exist.

And I'll do **anything** to beat him.

Luckily, I've got good at beating ol' George.

Enough is enough.

George Vanquist has ruined things for our family for the last time. He's a weaselly little shrimp, and we are mighty Bigfeet, after all. And I've got a plan. We are going to find Brian and bring him to this reunion. It's time he got over all of this. And now that it's settled, there's one totally essential, very important thing we have to do.

Let's pack!

Chapter 4:
YETI GETS READY

CASHEWS

BACK SCRATCHER

NEWT

UKULELE

FIRECRACKERS

BUG NET

GRANOLA OAT BARS

NOLEN

MEATBALL SUB

CURRENCY FROM TWENTY COUNTRIES

DRAGON COMPASS

Y-FRONTS

Oh, excuse me, let me introduce you to my assistants and best buddies, Alexander and Gunthar.

CRYPTOTRON

GUNTHAR
signed in

MERMAN
what is rain?

ABRA

EVIL
yum!

RALPH

O'BRIEN

Hi, I'm Alexander.

I work for Santa for four months a year. It's so **stressful**, Santa gives us an eight-month holiday.

But I **love** working, so in my time off, I work with Blizz. Our missions are the **most fun ever,** which is saying a lot since my other job is at the North Pole.

CRYPTOTR

cats on the

AUG

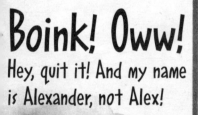

Last but **certainly** not least, my faithful hound, Frank the Arctic fox. He's got a lot of tricks up his sleeve.

BRITISH
COLUMBIA

CANADA
AMERICA

NEVADA

42

OK, so I'm all packed and ready to go.
Now it's time to head to Canada!
But we are going to need transportation.

I know just who to call!

FLY GUY

CALL

Hey there,

I'm Jack Saturday the unicorn. See this horn right here? It's a magic horn and it means... I can fly. Blizz is such an awesome dude. I'd do anything for him.

But have you ever flown to Canada with a **1,200-pound** yeti on your back?

45

Chapter 5:
ARRIVING IN CANADA

See you later, Blizz. Thanks for the generous burrito gift card. Call me anytime!

You're welcome, Jack! You've earned it!

Let me introduce you to my family. This is Marlon the skunk ape and that is Timmy the Sasquatch.

I'm sitting on a rock under a tree re-reading Harry Potter Book Six. It's a one-person job. Leave me alone. —

And that's...

Eddie

Torch

Kest

Mattman

Gregory

Groo

and Li'l Sherman.

But who sent the invitation?

Of course! Grandfather Goatman!

It was you, wasn't it, Grandpa?! I could tell it was your handwriting.

Yup, guilty!

So many of my best memories are from those reunions. But it won't be the same without Brian. I sure hope we can find him. Bigfeet, it's time to track him down!

Well, this might be a clue. It's a

"**big**" footprint

and a sprig of wild rosemary.
Brian has big feet and
loves to cook savoury dishes.
We're on the right track, guys!

*The Bigfeet don't know it, but not so
very far away, trouble is brewing...*

Chapter 6:
VANQUIST IN CANADA

··

George Vanquist here.

Richest and most famous

cryptozoologist in the world. Believe it or not, some people are still sceptical that Bigfoot exists, so I'm back here to get even more proof.

And to ensure my success I've brought ...

a state-of-the-art rocket bus ...

MOST EXPENSIVE
SURVEILLANCE
EQUIPMENT

VIDEO GAMES

WI-FI

LOO

George
VANQUIST
Crypto Specialist

HALOGEN
HEADLIGHTS

WRAP-AROUND FULL-COLOUR IMAGE

and Eagle Eye Z5000.

HD VIDEO
TOUCH SCREEN

700 MEGAPIXELS

MACRO
LENS

18.6MP DIGITAL SLR
DOUBLE-ZOOM LENS

NOODLES! What in the world is all this? Maps, maps, maps ... **you know I hate maps!**

Hmm, where is the parking brake on this thing? Where's my driver's licence? Where are the keys?

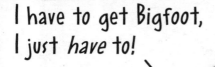

Chapter 7:
FIND BRIAN

• •

*Meanwhile, the Bigfeet are
also still looking for Brian.*

These Canadian woods
go on for ever! He could be
anywhere!

Wait,
I think I smell something!

Not here.

We've been looking for ever!

Not in this cave.

Do you know where?

BRIAN! It's you, you ol' Bigfoot! And you're roasting red potatoes with olive oil and rosemary. But I don't think you made enough to go around...

67

HOLY COW!

It's my whole family! You all probably hate me for getting caught and letting our secret out.

Brian, it wasn't your fault. It was an accident. We've all missed you so much. We love you, Bigfoot. Now that we've found you, let the family reunion begin!

We've got games, grub and good times ahead. Let's party like the crazy cryptids we are!

Alexander and Gunthar, I need you to stand guard. Look out for **sneaky photographers** who may try to take our picture. Here are some binoculars to help you spot them. REMEMBER, no one can find us. I'm counting on you guys to keep our secret safe and sound!

71

Look what you did!
How are we going to keep a lookout now?

Ugh, and get your feet
out of my face!

What's wrong with my feet?

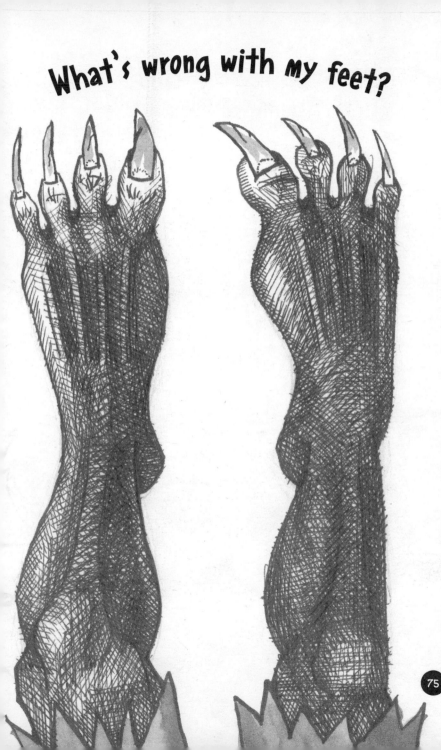

75

And later still...
... so Blizz stepped on the dragon's tail, but we got out in time!
I'm glad we met. Wanna go to a party?
It's just across the road.
George VANGST
Look who it is... Blizz isn't going to like this...

While Alexander and Gunthar are fighting, and Frank is making a new friend, Blizz and the family are partying hard. Too bad no one is watching out for evil cryptozoologists.

Chapter 8:
VANQUIST'S PROOF

Well, hello there.

I've successfully navigated us to British Columbia, Canada, to uncover the Bigfoot. No thanks to Noodles.

BEEP BEEP BEEP!

PARKING PERFECTLY

And I will not fail. I will get proof of Bigfoot.
Now I just have to find him!
Let's go. I know a shortcut...

Noodles,
why did you
lead me this way?
It's obviously wrong ...
cut me down!
NOW!

Did you like that, Noodles?

Leading me the wrong way to make a fool of me?

I know you think I'll never find Bigfoot again. And I've been patient with your fumbling so far. But if you don't shape up, your kind owner might not be so kind any more.

You were wrong. Noodles, you were wrong! I was right. I am the winner. You doubted me, Noodles. Shame on you!

Shame on you! You are one big dummy.
Now the world will have to agree that I'm
THE WORLD'S BEST CRYPTOZOOLOGIST!

89

Now take this camera and put it in my bag.
And don't mess this up ...

...or it's back to the pound with you.

I DID IT! I DID IT!

And once I download the photos to my system, the whole world will know I was right. In fact, I'm going to call every reporter and TV newsreader I know right now and give them the *scoop!*

That guy seems really **nasty.** You know, you don't have to put up with that kind of treatment!

Yeah! No one should be treated lik that. And you seem like a cool guy. What's your name?

Noodles. Y-y-you think I'm cool? No one has ever said that to me. With George Vanquist it's always "Find THIS, drive THERE, hold THAT..."
It's no fun!
You don't deserve that. Hmmm. I think I have an idea... Come with me!
WAIT!

Can I please have that camera?

This thing? Please take it. I'm not helping George any more. He's on his own!

I gotta get back to the reunion. Smell you later, buddies!
C'mon, Noodles. I think I know what to do to help you escape that awful owner of yours!

Chapter 10:
FRANK'S FINE FETCH

While George zooms away in the cryptomobile, Frank arrives at the reunion with a gift for Blizz.

It's a tie!
Guess we'll settle this next year.

Oh, hey, Frank! Who's a good boy? Whatcha got here? Is it a camera?
It's a camera!

"Property of George Vanquist"?

How did he get these shots? Did anyone else spot us? Alexander and Gunthar, do you know anything about this?

Chapter 10 ½:
VANQUIST TAKES A WRONG TURN

Noodles, these maps are all wrong!

Hmm... we seem to be in some sort of desert.
Beautiful, though. I think I'll take a picture.

Let me get my camera.

It's not here, I lost it.

Where am I? Who am I? Who are you? Why are we here? What is the meaning of life? Why is the sky blue? And why are those birds staring at me? Do they have my camera?

Chapter 11:
BACK AT HQ

Wow! I had a great time at the reunion. But it sure is nice to be home again. And I could use a long nap.

HOT DOG WITH COLESLAW

TROY THE ROBOT

ANCIENT ALIEN SKULL

Wow! What's this? A present?
We printed the pictures from Vanquist's camera. Just for us. You'll keep them safe from prying eyes, won't you?

As for the camera, it will never see the light of day again!

Frank, bury!

116

But first, we would like to welcome a new member to our team.

Noodles!